Waiting
for
Wings

Lois Ehlert

Harcourt, Inc.

San Diego   New York   London

Printed in Hong Kong

Out in
the fields,
eggs are
hidden
from view,

clinging
to leaves
with
butterfly
glue.

Soon
caterpillars
hatch. They
creep and chew.

Each one
knows what
it must do:

Find
a place
where
winds
don't
blow,

then
make
a case
in which
to grow.

Caterpillar
changes
now begin—

body
and
wings
take
shape
within.

When
it's time,
each case
is torn—

wings unfold;
new butterflies
are born!

They
pump
their wings,
get ready to fly,

then hungry
butterflies
head for the sky.

Looking for
flowers with
nectar to eat,

they catch
a whiff
of something
sweet.

They follow
that fragrant
scent of
perfume,

until
they
find
our
garden
in bloom.

We've been waiting for wings!

We watch them circle, land on their feet,

unroll their tongues, and begin to eat.

They
dip and sip,

then fly away,
back home
to the fields....

They have
eggs to lay.

Buckeye caterpillar food includes plantain leaves.

Buckeye underwings

Buckeye overwings

Buckeye
wingspan 2"–2½"

Buckeye chrysalis

Buckeye caterpillar

Monarch underwings

Tiger Swallowtail underwings

Painted Lady caterpillar food includes thistle leaves.

Painted Lady caterpillar

Painted Lady chrysalis

Painted Lady underwings

Painted Lady
wingspan 2"–2¼"

Painted Lady overwings

All of the objects in this book are illustrated at twice their actual size.

Butterfly Identification

Monarch
wingspan 3"–4"

Monarch caterpillar

Monarch chrysalis

Monarch overwings

Monarch caterpillars eat milkweed leaves.

Tiger Swallowtail caterpillar

Tiger Swallowtail chrysalis

Tiger Swallowtail
wingspan 3½"–6½"

Tiger Swallowtail overwings

Tiger Swallowtail caterpillar food includes cherry leaves.

Butterfly Information

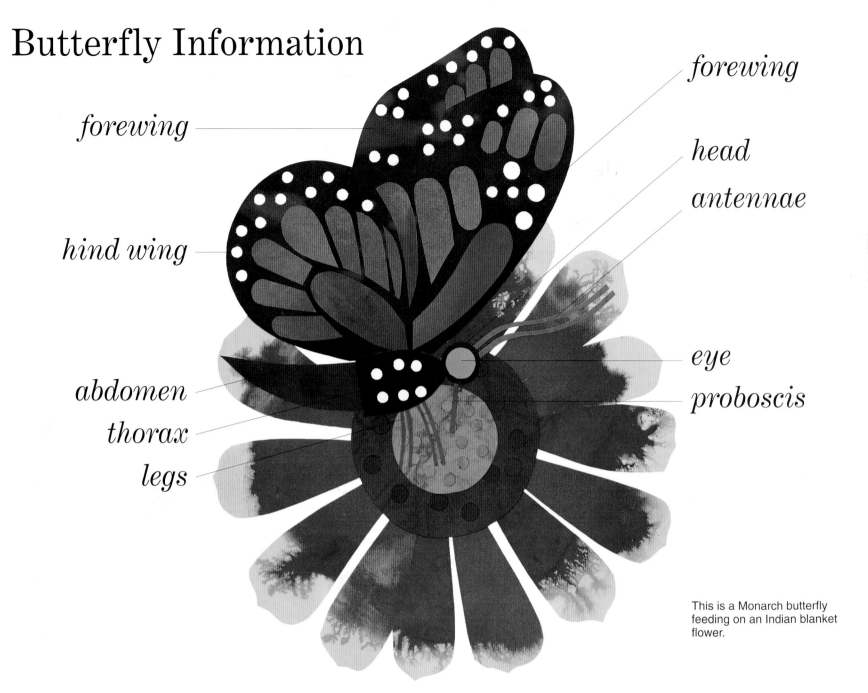

forewing

forewing

head

antennae

hind wing

eye

proboscis

abdomen

thorax

legs

This is a Monarch butterfly feeding on an Indian blanket flower.

What is a butterfly?

Butterflies are insects. Insects have six legs (although some butterflies, like the Monarch above, have underdeveloped forelegs), and they have three sections to their bodies: the head, the thorax, and the abdomen. A butterfly's four wings, as well as its legs, are attached to its thorax. Moths look similar to butterflies, but they are different. In most cases, butterflies have antennae with knobby tips, unlike moths, which have feathered antennae. Butterflies usually fly during the day; moths, mostly at night. When butterflies rest, they hold their wings above their backs; moths fold their wings flat over their backs.

How does a butterfly begin its life?

A butterfly begins its life as an egg laid by a female butterfly. When the egg hatches, a caterpillar emerges. The caterpillar spends most of its short life eating, but at a certain point it stops, attaches itself to a leaf or branch, and begins forming a protective case, called a chrysalis, around itself. Inside the chrysalis, the caterpillar develops into a butterfly. After a period of time, the case splits open and the butterfly emerges.

How does a butterfly eat?

Most butterflies feed on nectar, the sweet liquid secreted by flowers. A butterfly drinks the nectar through its proboscis, a linked pair of hollow, tongue-like tubes. The proboscis remains coiled up until the butterfly lands on a flower. Then the butterfly straightens out its proboscis until it resembles a pair of straws, and drinks the flower's nectar.

Flower Identification

hollyhock

impatiens

butterfly bush

zinnia

cosmos

Indian blanket flower or gaillardia

purple coneflower or echinacea

sweet william

flowering tobacco or nicotiana

verbena

pentas

phlox

lantana

marigold

black-eyed Susan

butterfly weed

Growing a Butterfly Garden

If you want to plant your own butterfly garden, start early, before the growing season begins. Find out which butterflies live in your area and which nectar-rich flowers will entice those butterflies to visit your garden. Generally butterflies are attracted to flowers of bright color and strong fragrance.

For ideas on what to plant, read books, including nature guides; study seed catalogs; and visit natural history museums. Explore as many public and private gardens as you can. Try to think like a butterfly! Don't be afraid to ask for advice from family and friends.

Make a list of flowers you'd like to plant, then visit a garden center. Read labels. Make sure the flowers on your list will grow in your area. Note how tall the flowers grow and when they will bloom. Try to plant flowers with varied heights and flowering cycles. Then make your selections and plant your butterfly garden.

When the flowers start to bloom, keep your eyes open and wait for wings. If you're lucky enough to have a butterfly visit your garden, stand quietly and enjoy its beauty.